# La Petit Refuge

Don Allen

ISBN:  979-8-9906053-8-1

eISBN: 979-8-9906053-7-4

Publisher: Don Allen

Also, by Don Allen

Sean Murphy Series
Satisfaction
Chaos
The Launderer
The Brotherhood
The Developer
Treasure
Assassination
Stolen Wealth
Phoenix

George Basdakis Series
Check for Junk
The Gurkha
Gold Mine
Cousin

Sam Goodwin Series
Dog Walker
The Irishmen
The Congressman
Kidnapped

Joseph Barszcz
La Petit Refuge

**In memory of Joe Panek
(1916-2012)**

Tales told here may or may
not reflect his actual
experiences, but he would
have liked the story.

<u>Special acknowledgment:</u>

The characters of Harvey Bains and Jane
were borrowed from the British sitcom
*Waiting for God,* which ran on the BBC
from 1990 to 1994

# 1  La Petit Refuge

I'm Joseph Barszcz, known as JB. to my friends. I'll be ninety-four next month. I never thought I'd make it this far. My father and his father checked out in their seventies. But I'm not complaining -- except for my recent medical issues. I'm a retired homicide detective, retired thirty years ago. I was with the Hartford Police Department for thirty years, followed by my time with *Security One, Inc.*, a contractor providing security at Bradley International Airport. Prior to this, I was in the Army Air Corps, serving a good portion of my WWII years in England as an aircraft mechanic.

I'm first-generation American-Polish. My parents immigrated in 1902 from the Austria-Hungary province of Galicia. Today, their village, Ropica, is located in Poland.

I was born in 1916. Stella was the oldest of my seven siblings; I was number six in the pecking order. Stella became a surrogate mother to Andrew, the youngest, and me. Poppa and Momma worked six days a week in the Ludlow jute mill.

While in England, I was the unit's boxing champ. Standing at six feet three inches in my stocking feet and weighing in at over two hundred thirty pounds put me in the heavyweight division. I was unbeaten by American challengers. Then there was 'the Scott,' Robin MacHeath from the Royal Highland Fusiliers. He was close to seven feet tall. Hitting him was like hitting a brick wall. When I came to after our first and last match, I recall him saying, *'That was just a wee tap laddie.'*

I met Audry, the love of my life, in 1950. We were married in '53. To both our regrets, we were never able to have children. Audry would not consider adoption, claiming you never knew what you'd get. Her older cousin adopted an infant boy years ago. He was always in trouble, first at school and, as he got older, with the police. He was later diagnosed as being schizophrenic, a genetic disorder, the doctors said.

Over the years, as a substitute for our own children, we became close to my sister Stella's children, Joe and Barbara.

In our later years, Audry and I vacationed frequently in Florida, trying to decide on a retirement location. The West Palm Beach area appeared to be the least impacted by annual hurricanes. We settled on Jamaica Bay, a retirement community in Boynton Beach. It was a trailer park community where half the residents went north for the summers. We bought a twelve hundred square foot unit with two bedrooms, two baths, a living room, a dining room, and a kitchen. We later added a ten-by-thirty sun porch.

Audry died in 2001. It was a tough time. My niece, Barb and her husband, visited several times, both before and after

Audry's passing. During one extended visit on her own, Barb helped me adjust to my new life. All was going well until three years ago when my neighbor found me passed out on the kitchen floor. He first called 911 and then my niece.

Frances Nadeau, my neighbor, a retired fireman in his seventies was from Enfield, Connecticut. He was a widower. His wife had friends living at Jamaica Bay and she had made arrangements for them to move there several years ago before her passing. John carried through with her plan and moved into the adjacent trailer five years ago. Frances , at first, was a bit standoffish, but over time we became good friends.

The doctors didn't give me a specific diagnosis but strongly suggested I not live alone. I gave Barb my power of attorney. Her mission, find me a new home. The Hospital Ombudsman referred her to a couple of local retirement communities. Both were beautiful, provided lovely services, and were well beyond my means. My doctor wanted to discharge me before Barb found a new home. He strongly recommended that I not return to Jamaica Bay, where I would live alone.

One of the senior nurses pulled Barb aside, "The Hospital gets a kickback from those fancy retirement communities. Try *La Petit Refuge*. Don't tell the staff here that I recommended it."

*La Petit Refuge* was affordable. My pension and social security covered expenses, leaving a reasonable excess for me to squander on wine, women, and song – well, I can always dream, can't I?

*La Petit Refuge* turned out to be an old Radisson Inn that had been repurposed into a retirement home for approximately 175 seniors. It was located on Rt. 1, two blocks from the Inland Coastal Waterway, four blocks from the Atlantic Ocean, and sandwiched between West Palm Beach and Boca Raton. In other words, the Inn was in a tourist dead zone.

*La Petit Refuge's* residents were middle-class senior citizens. Most financially secure but not rich, in reasonably good health, but unable to live an independent lifestyle. A few still had their cars; most relied on walkers or canes.

There were two types of rooms at the retirement home: a basic 15x20 hotel room. Or the deluxe hotel room, 15x30, the additional ten feet, which in the day, was advertised as a sitting area. Barb chose the latter, and in time, I really appreciated the additional space. My recliner and side table sat at one end, and my new 42" Sony TV on a chest of drawers at the other end. A small stuffed chair for visitors was accommodated in between.

# 2 The First Day

"Okay Uncle Joe, let's get going. I've arranged for an ambulance to take you to the retirement home. The staff here won't let me drive you."

"Tell the bloody doctor I'll drive myself," I said, knowing it would never happen. I knew my driving days were over since I was subject to fainting spells.

Barb was using my Crown Vic while she was in Florida. I asked her to sell the car before returning home next week; I didn't need the temptation sitting in the parking lot. There had already been two calls asking about it. I'd get the nine thousand I was asking.

Barb was waiting for me when the ambulance arrived at the retirement home. An aide assisted me out of the ambulance and into the waiting wheelchair. Barb wheeled me into the *La Petit Refuge's* lobby, where we were met by a well-dressed man, probably in his 40s, medium height and weight, and with slicked-back black hair.

As he stepped forward to meet us, "Mr. Barszcz, welcome to the *La Petit Refuge of Boynton Beach.* Your niece has been telling us about you. We are here to make your stay as pleasant as possible. I'm Harvey Bains, the manager of this 'zoo' and will see that you are well looked after. I'm here to help you adjust. Jane here, Jane, where are you?" he says, looking around, "is my assistant. She can answer your questions." Jane is a mousy little lady wearing a gray cardigan despite the summer temperature.

Barbara tells me you are coming from Jamaica Bay. Several of our residents lived there; perhaps you know some of them."

"I think Betty Stuart may be one," I mumbled.

"Yes, she's on the third floor of the south wing. You might see her at dinner tonight."

"Well, Jane's here to answer your questions, but I suggest you first ask Leroy Williams; he's our daytime concierge. He knows more about what is going on here than most of us on the management team, including me."

"Leroy," Harvey called out. A slim black man in his early 30s stepped out from behind the reception desk.

"Yes sir, boss," he said.

"Leroy, quit clowning and come over and meet our new resident, Joseph Barszcz. I think you have already met his niece, Barbara Zych. He will be in Apartment N432. Please help him get settled in."

"And now, if you'll excuse me, I have other duties I must attend to," said Harvey.

After Harvey had left, Leroy properly introduced himself and said, "Welcome to the *La Petit Refuge*. I'll do what I can to help you settle in. I think your niece has had your furniture moved in and your apartment prepared for you."

As Leroy started wheeling me down the hall, he was saying, "You have to take Harvey with a grain of salt; he can be somewhat of a twit at times. You are in apartment N432, that's in the north wing. The elevator is in the middle of the wing, next to the stairwell. There is also a stairwell at the end of the hall to be used in case of fire."

As Leroy pushed me to the elevator, he pointed out the community room that was used for social gatherings, the study where some of the men had coffee each morning, and the dining room. When we arrived at my 'new' home, he handed me a folder. Here is some information on *La Petit Refuge,* dining times, description of services provided, and contact numbers. "To get me, just enter '0' when asked for the house extension. I'll leave you two now. Dinner service starts at five."

I was still in a daze from my medication. Looking around, I saw what I thought to be a pleasant room, a pleasant room for a hotel. But as Barb explained, my finances were limited. The room had the extended space to accommodate my recliner, side table, and TV, with space for a small stuffed chair for visitors. There was a small alcove nestled in between two closets providing a mini kitchen: a small fridge and a microwave. The closets provided minimal storage space. To the left of the bed was the bathroom, which had been modified to assist the handicapped, I guess that included me now, and to the right, a half wall separating my 'sitting room' from the 'bedroom.' Barb had used the space between the half wall and my bed to store a few boxes of 'stuff,' which she directed me to sort through and determine the content's final disposition.

Barb and I were late in getting down to dinner. I have no idea of what was served. Leroy promised to introduce me to my fellow 'inmates' tomorrow when my head was clearer.

Back in 432, after getting me in bed, Barb reminded me I had a doctor's appointment in the morning and that she would be back by eight to get me ready. "I'll ask the doctor about different medications. I can't leave you in this befuddled state."

"I'm leaving now," Barb said. "This will be the last night I can stay in your trailer. Frances has arranged a cleaning crew to tackle it tomorrow. Goodwill is picking up all the remaining furniture first thing in the morning. And Frances tells me Jamaica Bay management may have a prospective buyer for your trailer."

"I've booked a room at the Marriott Courtyard. Monday, I have to go home."

# 3  Bomba de Mierda[1]

My doctor's appointment that Thursday resulted in him telling me I looked great – for a nonagenarian. He agreed that the medication I was on was no longer needed. The hospital doctors had overprescribed the narcotic.

"I'm surprised you can get around. The dose prescribed is enough for a man twice your size. You should be thinking more clearly by the end of the day," Dr. Wilkins said.

Leroy met us in the lobby with a wheelchair. While helping me, he said, "For dinner tonight, I've seated you with some men you might find interesting."

Wheeling me down the hallway to the elevator, Barb parked me in the mini lobby by the elevator. "I'll be right back, Uncle Joe. I think Leroy has a package for you, something I ordered last night."

As she left, my bowels started rumbling. I have not had a good bowel movement in days. I may be in a narcotic daze, but my body functions worked. Thinking I was on the fourth floor,

---

[1]  Shit Bomb

why else would I be sitting by the elevator? I got up and stumbled down the hall to my room, or what should have been my room, room number N432.

The four was kind of blurry in hindsight; it could have been one. The door was unlocked. As I entered, I could feel liquid oozing down my leg. I had to get to the bathroom!! Just as I got my shorts down, my backside exploded. Too late now, I fumbled for the light switch. Audry's comb and brush were by the sink. What were they doing there? OMG, I realized I was in the wrong apartment. Using the towels hanging there, a little more damage at this point wouldn't hurt; I cleaned myself up the best I could and stumbled back into the hallway just as Barb was coming down with the wheelchair.

"Uncle Joe, where did you go?"

I pointed to the apartment I just came out of and said, "I had an accident."

Looking at me and the brown trail on the floor, she said, "Let's get you upstairs."

We were able to get to my apartment without meeting anyone. Barb got me into the shower, handed me soap and a washcloth, and told me to get cleaned up while laying out a new set of clothes for me. My old clothes went into a trash bag that was double sealed in a second trash bag.

Sitting in my recliner, I was embarrassed reflecting on what had happened. The one positive outcome was that my thoughts were no longer hazy.

"I've got to tell Leroy what happened," I said.

"Later, get some sleep now," directed my niece.

*** 

That afternoon, I was using my walker as Barb and I headed down to the main lobby for my confession. On the way, we passed two of the housecleaning staff, and, to my chagrin, I overheard them.

"Did you hear about the mess in Agnes's apartment? A '*bomba de mierda.*' Rosa tells me there were even flecks on the ceiling," said the first woman.

"Agnes is mortified – she's thinking some may think it was her. And the mess, even the towels were soiled," said the second.

Looking straight ahead, I pressed forward, my face turning red with embarrassment.

Getting to the front desk, Leroy was joking around. "The 'phantom shitter' has returned," he is saying to another resident. "Every six months or so, someone has a massive accident. He or she hit N132 this morning. The cleaning staff tells me it was the most amazing accident to date."

Hearing this, Barb grips my elbow and suggests we step outside to sit in the sun for a while.

"Let it go, Uncle Joe; there is nothing to be gained from your confession. Accidents of this type appear to be commonplace here, and taking ownership of today's event will only lead to you being accused of every future event."

# 4 The Geezers

After my explosive entry into the Refuge, Leroy hosted Barb and me in the dining room, where he introduced several of the residents. Don't ask me their names; it was too many people at one time for my poor mind to absorb. Several became good friends as time passed.

That first dinner, Leroy placed Barb and me at a table and told us how the dining room worked. "There is a steam line, much like those found in a military mess hall. You walk down the line and point to what you want. There is usually a choice of two or three entries. The attendant places your choice on a plate that you have on the tray you are pushing along."

"And how do I get the try to the table? I asked.

"At the end of the line are dining room attendants. The attendants help you with your tray, taking it to your table for you. They also performed basic waitering duties such as getting you coffee."

"The dining room attendants," he said, "are from the *Culinary Institute*, a trade school only a few blocks away that we have contracted with. In essence, the *Culinary Institute* is

13

paid to manage our dining facility while using it as part of their educational program. The attendants get course credits and are paid fifteen dollars an hour, tax-free. Each can earn up to a thousand dollars a month, the cap imposed by the school. The program is extremely popular with the students."

Leroy went on, "Some of the attendants and residents, mostly the women, form attachments much like parent and child. That could be because many of the students come from broken homes or have been placed in the Institute as an alternative to jail time."

Great, I'm thinking served by would be criminals.

*** 

Two weeks later, I found myself in the 'study,' a space adjacent to the formal dining room overlooking the lobby where old men gathered daily for coffee and gossip. I joined the group at Leroy's insistence. They called themselves 'the Geezers.' Several of the members were originally from the Northeast, moving to Florida with their wives a decade or more ago to retire in the sun as Audry and I had done. Most were now widowers. Ages ranged from the low eighties to the high nineties. I fit right in.

They were initially intrigued by my background as a homicide detective. They wanted the juicy details of murders and mayhem. I disappointed them as I explained, "Most of my time with the Hartford Police Department was spent on mundane tasks, mostly administrative. Most of the murders I handled were domestic, with each resulting in hours of paperwork. But there was one that I can tell you about, *the tobacco murders*."

"Shade tobacco is a big crop in central Connecticut. The work is seasonal, with farms bringing in Jamaican and Puerto Rican workers. The two groups don't mix well. When farms are adjacent to each other, Jamaicans on one and Puerto Ricans on the other, there is often trouble. Fist fights and stabbings are the norm. And an occasional murder that I would get involved with when the local jurisdiction sought our help."

"One year, there was a particularly gruesome murder. A young Puerto Rican was found gutted and wrapped in shade netting. The Enfield Police Department asked for our help. The case was assigned to me. I had no clues to work with. The farm managers had a hell of a time that summer containing the Puerto Ricans who wanted revenge. At the end of the season, all the migrant workers went home. Everyone, my Chief included, blamed me for not solving the case. It was a long winter with assignments, not much better than traffic control."

"At the start of the following year, a similar murder happened. Another Puerto Rican corpse. This time I was able to catch the murderer. He left a bloody switchblade behind. Not only did it have his fingerprints, but his initials were carved into the handle. In three days, I had the culprit. I got a big write-up in the local papers. The mayor of Enfield was ecstatic.

And all my Chief said, 'Why didn't you do this last September.'"

The others had their stories to tell, probably not for the first time. In time, I would probably repeat *the tobacco murderer* story. Politics were occasionally discussed but not passionately. We all knew politicians spun promises to get votes. Sports tended to dominate our discussions, with the exception of the physical attributes of some of the visiting nurses – we're old but not dead.

Later, Jeb, a lobsterman from Gloucester, organized a deep-sea fishing outing. Five of us went. I didn't catch anything other than a sunburn.

Other outings the group organized were trips to jai alai games and the greyhound races. I still hear Sammy, *Sammy the bookie*, originally from New Jersey, saying, 'trust me, we can make a score here.' Someday, I'll learn not to bet on games I don't know anything about. Now, when we went to the horse track, I recouped my earlier losses.

One of the more interesting characters was Tony. He looked like Danny DeVito, and to top it off, he was a former taxi cab dispatcher. He was from Boston. He tried hard to imitate Louie De Palma from the TV show *Taxi*.

Pete was a former photojournalist. He was more than happy to share old photos he took for *Sports Illustrated* – the rejected ones he took for the swimsuit editions. He still dabbled on the side, working local ethnic festivals.

To the extent the Geezers had a leader, it would have been Gerald. Gerald Goldstein was a former small-time comic who played clubs in the Catskills. He never made it big, only one or two walk-on roles in the movies. But he would keep us in stitches – his impression of Harvey was priceless.

# 5 Publix

Shortly after moving into *La Petit Refuge,* I noticed the snacks Barb stocked up for me were depleted. There was a Publix grocery store just up the street. It would be no problem to walk there, especially with my new Rollator Walker. If I got tired, I could always sit. I had my morning outing planned.

With handicap-accessible curbs, I had no problem. The walk took less than ten minutes. Publix must get a lot of business from *La Petit Refuge*; they had specially adapted carts that attached to walkers.

As I cruised through the store, I had to keep reminding myself I could only manage two small plastic bags with my Rollator. I restricted my purchases to what I knew I could manage. Leaving the store, a black youth who looked like a local gangbanger, asked if I needed any help. "Ya, right," and I told him to get lost.

Back at the retirement home, I told Leroy about my Publix experience.

"Two years ago," said Leroy, "my nephew was hit by a car out front on the main road. Yes, he was running from the police, but put that aside. My sister didn't have the means to care for him. When the residents here learned he was my nephew, they took up a collection for him. Up to that point, the gang he ran with harassed our residents. After that, it's as if they adopted the tenants. On more than one occasion, they have run off encroaching gangs who were threatening our people. They help with grocery bags, and yes, maybe they solicit tips, but they help."

Now I felt bad; I had to make this right. I asked Leroy to look after my two bags and returned to the store. My gangbanger was still idling in front of the store. Going over to him, "I'm sorry for my curt reply. As you can probably guess, I'm from the retirement home just up the street. I'm new there. Leroy just told me about the history of your gang and the home. I look forward to any help you offer me in the future."

"I understand," he said. "I'd probably freak to if a stranger popped up offering me help. Especially if he had spiky yellow hair like mine. My name is Terance. I'm called 'T.' Where you all from?"

"I'm Joseph Barszcz. My friends call me JB. I used to live in the Jamaica Bay trailer park, but doctors felt I shouldn't live by myself anymore. So here I am at *La Petit Refuge*."

"And where did you live before that?" T asked.

"You are full of questions. Before I lived in Hartford. I was a police officer."

I could see T tightening up, "But not to worry," I said. "I was a homicide detective. You not hiding any bodies, are you?"

T laughed and offered a fist bump, "Okay JB, you're cool."

# 6  A Body, Mabey

The Geezers were in the midst of their daily discussion, mostly a few comments here and there, followed by silence. Gerald, to get the conversation going observed, "I haven't seen Charlie recently. His aide comes and goes, the TV blares away, and diner trays are left by his door, but where is Charlie? Now, I could have used this for one of my skits – a nursing aide in a retirement home does not report the death of her patient. Instead, she moves into the patient's apartment, uses his bank account, which is replenished monthly, and gets free meals."

"And no one in the home misses him?  Not a realistic storyline," said Pete. "Now, you could have him run off with the nursing aide. That might work; she is kind of cute."

As the banter is going back and forth discussing the merits of Charlie's aide, I noticed Betty Stuart rushing into the lobby heading for Bains's office. I haven't seen her move that fast with her walker since she had won at Jamaica Bay's bingo night. She was clearly flustered.

"Excuse me," I told my fellow Geezers, "I think Betty might need some help."

As I got to her, Harvey rushed out of his office to intercept her, not wanting a scene in front of 'his' people. I heard her telling Harvey in a panicked voice, "Harvey, there's a body on the third floor just outside my door,"

"Now, now Betty, are you really sure? It could be no more than some laundry someone dropped," and under his breath, "or a shadow."

Betty did have early-onset dementia and was known to be confused at times.

"No! I saw a foot on the floor sticking out of the door to the stairwell!!"

"Calm down, Betty. I'll call Rudy to check the stairwell; he's changing lights in the stairwell," Harvey said and turned to the receptionist's desk to make a call while Leroy looked on. After a few words, he turned back to Betty, "Rudy said he found an old rag someone was using to prop the door open. Everything is fine. While you are down here, why don't you get some coffee and a pastry," Harvey said condescendingly as he motioned over one of the house staff to lead the now confused woman into the dining room.

Standing with Leroy after Harvey was gone, Leroy remarked, "That was an amazing call. Harvey was holding down the receiver cradle with his finger. I wonder what his game is now?"

"I'm going to wander up by Betty's room to have a look," I said.

"Suggest you not stir the pot," he said with some seriousness.

Taking the south elevator to the third floor, I stepped into the hallway and – no body. The door to the stairwell was closed. At the door, I noticed scuff marks on the rug; the nap was lying the wrong way. Opening the door, I saw what looked like blood drops on the landing. A blood trail led down the stairs. Leaving my walker in the hallway, I managed to go down the stairs using the hand railings. The blood dribbles went to the first floor and out into the parking lot, where they stopped. *Was there a body? Was it placed in a vehicle?* were my first thoughts.

"Hay you, what are you doing here?" came the question from a burly guy just stepping out from between the two new Cadillac sedans.

Playing for time, I gave him a confused look, asking, "Where's the lobby? My daughter is taking me out for lunch. Have you seen my cane?" As I continued to mumble, he threw up his hands. "Butch, another inmate has escaped; take him back to the front."

A younger man came up beside me; he was wearing a sports coat, and if I didn't know better, it was concealing a shoulder holster. "This way, old man," he said as he not so gently led me back into the building and the first-floor hallway. "Coming through, boss, I have to escort this gent to the front," he called out.

The hallway looked like an extension of the apartments, a sofa here, a stuffed chair there, and apartment doors ajar, extensions to the long room. At the other end was another door that opened to the south elevator's mini lobby. Earlier, on my way up, I hadn't noticed this door. He escorted me by my elbow back to the main lobby.

# 7  The Andrew Sisters

Butch deposited me in the lobby as Leroy looked on.

"I see you met the folks in the back," said Leroy. "They'll be watching you now."

"Who the hell are they, and what's with the first floor of the south wing? It looks like one large apartment."

"The owner of the *La Petit Refuge* lives there, or at least that's what I've been told. He moved in about the time I started here; that would be ten years ago."

"Residents living on the first floor of that wing were moved to other apartments, some unwillingly, even with the financial inducement of the waiver of three-month rent."

"The fire marshal took exception when they attempted to close the alley in the back of the building by placing two of those storage pods in the middle of the lane. They had to get rid of one; the other now sits by the rear fence. I think it's being used as some kind of workshop; it has power and a window air conditioner placed in an opening cut into one side."

"There was also another fire code violation when they installed the door blocking off half of the south wing's first floor. Next time you're back that way, notice the enlarged elevator lobby and the new building exit to the right of it. The fire marshal required that modification before approving the closure of the hallway with doors."

He went on, "Wednesday nights, the old man is usually wheeled into the theater for the night's entertainment. At his request, we have a standing booking with the Palm Beach Arts Society for groups replicating performers from the '40s. This week it's the *Andrew Sister's Look-Alikes*. He normally gets there after the show starts, sits in the back and leaves as the show finishes. If you want to see him, be there by eight and sit in the back on the left side of the theater."

"And Butch with a shoulder holster?" I asked.

"They must have big rats in the alley," said Leroy.

That Wednesday, I was in the theater at the time Leroy suggested and had a seat in the back row. The lighting was not particularly good, so I hoped I wouldn't be recognized when Butch pushed a wheelchair into its reserved space. In the chair was a wizened old man who made me look ten years younger. Under the wrinkles, there was something familiar – I could not put my finger on it.

As for the *Andrew Sister's Look-Alikes,* they were good; they gave me flashbacks from sixty years ago.

\*\*\*

For the next several weeks, I pretty much minded my own business, with one exception. A body was found in one of the canals not far from the retirement home –not long after my adventures in the south wing.

I knew one of the guys on the Palm Beach police force; we played golf together on weekends before my knees started giving me trouble. On a hunch, I decided to call him,

"Randy, how's your game? If they let me play, I'd still beat you, even hobbling around with my walker ... Yes, I'm fine, but I have a question. I read in the paper that the PBPD pulled a body, partially eaten by alligators, out of a canal last week. Can you tell me anything about it? ... No, it's just a hunch I'm playing with; I don't have any leads for you. ... Okay, thanks. If I think of anything, I'll call."

Well, that was interesting. Randy's information was that the body was identified as Emilio Rodriguez, a New York City lowlife. A member of the Puerto Rican crime family.

# 8  Where is Johnny?

Late one afternoon I found the lobby in turmoil. Leroy was trying to get the attention of the residents who were milling about. "People, people, please calm down!" he was yelling. "We will find him!"

Pulling Leroy aside, "Find who?"

With a flustered look, he says, "John Wilson. He was last seen at breakfast when he told his table mates he was going out for a walk. He hasn't been seen since."

John was one of the more senior residents. He was still in relatively good physical health, although he did need a walker to get around. Over the past few months, his cognitive abilities appeared to be deteriorating. His daughter was there that afternoon to take him to a doctor's appointment to be evaluated."

"Have you notified the local authorities?" I asked.

"No, Harvey squashed that idea saying it would reflect badly on the home. He wants to wait a bit longer, saying John will turn up any time now."

Looking across the lobby, I saw a flustered Harvey arguing with a middle-aged lady, clearly not a resident, who had her phone out and was making a call. She was punching in numbers as Harvey was shaking his head.

I knew John slightly. He was a nice enough fellow, often without much to say. He was a platoon sergeant with the 101st Airborne, one of the men who parachuted into France on D-day. He seldom talked about his combat experiences, but they clearly left a mark on him. He occasionally sat in with the Geezers.

I walked out to the street, wondering where he could have gone. Pushing my walker down the street toward Publix, I found T helping one of the residents with a bag of stuff.

"JB, where is your Rollator? You're not going to carry much with your walker."

"One of the residents is missing. You haven't seen John Wilson, have you?"

"Johnny, no. He hasn't been to Publix in the past six months. He usually calls me every few weeks, and I get stuff for him. He's missing?"

"He hasn't been seen since the morning," I said.

"Leroy called the police?"

"No, Harvey is holding off, thinks it will reflect badly on the Refuge.

"Something wrong with that man," said T. "Johnny's a good guy; I'll get some of the boys to spread out and look for him as soon as I get Mrs. Meekins here into the lobby."

As T walked Mrs. Meekins into the lobby, a PBPD squad car pulled into the parking lot. Randy was driving; getting out, he came over to me, "I hear you lost one of the inmates. I was the only one in the squad room; the Captain asked me to check it out -- maybe another one of your bodies?"

"Like the one you found in the canal," I retorted.

I went on to explain what was happening. I saw a twinkle in his eye. "Come with me?" We get inside, and he asks which one is Harvey Bains.

"Mr. Bains, I understand you've lost a resident," Randy started "and delayed calling in the authorities. If anything has happened to Mr. Wilson, I'll be charging you with senior neglect."

As Harvey turns white, Randy turns to Leroy and gets a description of John. "Mind if I use your phone?" he asked. When the call was answered, "Maybel, this is Officer Tyler; please connect me with Missing Persons. One of the residents at the *La Petit Refuge* has wandered off; we need to find him before dark." After a little more talk, Randy turned to Leroy, "Patrol cars will be scouring the area. We will find him."

"Although I can't do anything, you can tell your esteemed boss that you thought you overheard me recommending to my

Captain that charges should be filed. That should tighten up his shorts."

I called T to tell him the police had joined the search. "If any of your boys find Johny, they should flag down a police car if they see one."

About an hour later Randy is bringing John into the lobby. Jojo, one of T's boys, is with them.

"Jojo found Mr. Wilson on the beach, just sitting watching the waves," Randy said.

John's daughter rushed over and hugged him. "Dad, I was so worried; why did you wander off?"

Looking somewhat confused, "your mother always loved the beach. I just wanted to see it one more time."

Two weeks later, John Wilson was dead. He didn't have dementia or Alzheimer's. It was an undetected cancer in the brain. Did he have a premonition?

# 9 Surveillance

I had not given up on the missing body mystery. On two occasions, I questioned Harvey about the residents on the first floor of the south wing. *'you don't need to worry about them, was his reply.'* When asked who they were and why they had an armed aide, he became more agitated, telling me, *'Mind your own business if you knew what was good for you.'*

Now, I don't take good to threats, and my curiosity was aroused.

I decided to solicit help from the Geezers. "I told you guys about the body Betty thought she saw and Harvey's evasive answers to my questions. I'd like to collect some information on our neighbor in the south wing. Do any of you know him or have ever talked with him?"

"No," was the collective reply.

One of the Geezers, Pete, the former photojournalist, had the end room on the fourth floor of the north wing, overlooking the back alleyway. "Pete, would you mind setting up your camera and getting a photo record of the comings and goings in the back alley?"

"Not at all. This is the most excitement I've had since Johnny, rest his soul, went missing."

That afternoon, we set his camera up, "We want license plate numbers and face shots. Keep the blinds down and shoot between the slats. I don't want them to see you."

Three days later, the Geezers were reviewing the photos Pete took. We had two new cars, Lincoln Town Cars, both with New York plates, parked out back for one night. We had photos of Butch and his older crony, Leim, as well as the drivers of the two cars. And of what appeared to be a senior 'boss' getting out of the rear of one of the cars.

"Pete, these are excellent photos," I said. "The faces are almost good enough for a police lineup." That was not far off the mark.

Later that week, I asked Randy to come by the residence; "I might have something of interest," I told him.

When he arrived, I invited him to join the Geezers for coffee in the 'study' and then explained what we had. "Randy, we've been doing a bit of snooping on our friends down the hall. Here are some photos of two cars, New York plates, and some nice face shots. I know for sure that the guy in the plaid sports coat has a shoulder holster. Now, back in the day, when I was a detective with the Hartford police, I would have tagged these guys as possible mobsters."

Randy looks up with a smile on his face, "And you want me to run them in on your gut feelings? Not today, thank you."

"No, no, you misunderstand. What I'm suggesting is you run the plates and see who they belong to, and as for the faces, you might contact your New York counterpart to see if these people are known to them."

About then, Harvey wanders in, sees the photos, and notices Randy sitting at the table, "Officer, you're not going to threaten me with bogus charges again, are you." Turning to me, "Joe, what are the pictures for?"

"Well, perhaps you can shed some light on them. We all know Butch. Who are the other men? These two cars spent the night here. Do you know whose they are?"

"Joe, I told you to leave this alone," Harvey said. "I can't be responsible for whatever happens to you."

"That sounds like a threat, Mr. Bains. Care to elaborate?" said Randy.

And poor Harvey went into his *hum, hum, hum* stammer.

# 8   Charlie

One bright fall day, I was shooting the breeze with Leroy. "Think the hot weather is gone?" I asked him.

"No, weather here is fickled; will come back and slap you upside your head. I've seen years, well into the fall months, and we get hit by a string of days in the high nineties. And then, the next day, you're looking for that sweater you packed away last spring."

As we're chatting, a young man in his late twenties comes over to the concierge desk. "Good morning, I'm Buz Zimerman; I'm here to see Charlie Zimmerman; I'm his grandson. My parents have not heard from him in several months and are getting a bit worried. I'm a co-pilot with Delta Airlines. I promised to look in on him the next time I was in Miami."

"Good morning," said Leroy, "Let's see if he is in." Leroy called Charlie's room; the aide answered. "Maybelline, this is the front desk," said Leroy. "Charlie's grandson is in the lobby and would like to come up for a visit ... Okay, give us a call when he is ready."

Leroy turns to Buz. Charlie is still in bed. Maybelline is going to get him dressed. Maybelline is his aide. She'll call me when he's ready, maybe ten minutes."

Five minutes later, Pete comes through the lobby door. "Who lit a fire under Maybelline? She must have been hittin a hundred-ten when her Cadillac left the parking lot."

Buz and I look at Leroy. "We should take a look," Leroy says as he takes the master key out of the top drawer.

Charlie's room is S210. We found the door locked. Leroy opens it with the passkey. The room is orderly, with a bag of trash by the door to be taken out, the bed made, and the TV on in the extended area; Charlie's room was a mirror of mine. Walking into the room, Buz sees one of those sealable plastic mattress covers between the bed and the half wall. It's not empty.

My years as a homicide detective kicked in, "Don't touch it!" Moving my walker over to the end of the bed, I take one of Charlie's canes and pull back a corner of the cover. Charlie's dead eyes are staring at us. "Out of the room, don't touch anything," I said as I led the two out into the hall. "Lock the door. We need to call the police."

The PBPD responds, and of course, it's Randy as the officer in charge. "JB, not another body," he says as he approaches the desk. Seeing the grave looks on our faces, he drops his sense of humor, "Okay, what's going on?"

We tell him what we found and of Maybelline's hasty departure. He makes a quick call and requests an APB for Maybelline's Cadillac, then asks to be shown to Charlie's room.

After the coroner has removed the body and the police have secured the room, Harvey comes out of his office. "Mr. Baines care to explain?" Randy asks. "Last month, you had a missing resident; this month, you have a dead resident." Poor Harvey, he's flustered and tongue-tied -- not normal for Harvey. "As you can probably guess, I'll be reporting this to the county's Senior Citizen Housing Commission." Harvey turns white. Jane keeps him from collapsing, walking him over to a chair.

Later, Pete is telling the Geezers that as Charlie's body is being removed, the fleeting glimpses he caught of the south wing, first floor feelings were that of trepidation as police vehicles took over the alleyway.

# 9 FBI

We're sitting around the 'Geezer table' when Pete asks, "Did I see a rescue vehicle here early this morning during my walk?"

"Yes," answered Gerald. "Jimmy in N204 took another fall in the middle of the night. The aide found him sprawled out in the bathroom this morning. He wasn't wearing his fall detector. The rescue team thinks he hit his head on the commode and may have a concussion. They took him to St. Mary's Medical Center. It was the only facility opened with a staffed ER that early in the morning. Leroy is trying to get his status."

As we drifted back into silence, I mentioned Randy called yesterday. "The two Town Cars we saw are registered with the Kinahan Cartel, and the older gent is Eddie 'the blade' Boyle."

"What the hell is the Kinahan Cartel," Jeb asked.

"Apparently, they are a branch of the Irish mob," I said. "Perhaps you've found some of their handy work when tending your lobster traps," I joked. "You've heard the term, 'sleeping with the fishes.'"

"Eddie is on the NYPD watch list, but no outstanding warrants. Oh, Butch is also on their watch list; he's a foot solder."

As the conversation hit another lull, we noticed two men in dark suits entering the lobby.

"I'll bet my pension those are FBI agents," I said. Notice how their suits are tailored to conceal their weapons."

"What weapons?" said someone.

"Exactly."

Leroy had a short conversation with them and then pointed across the lobby to the administration office, where Harvey had a small office. He did not have time to give Harvey a heads-up.

Soon after the agents entered the office, Jane and the bookkeeper appeared to have been ejected and were now clustered around Leroy's concierge desk. Gerald, stepping into the lobby, called them over.

"Jane, what's happening?" was our first collective question.

Ted pulled up two chairs for the ladies and offered to get them coffee, which was declined.

Jane was always in a frazzled state, but now she was a basket case. "FBI agents are integrating Harvey," she whimpered. "He hasn't done anything."

"That's true; he never does," was one remark I heard under someone's breath.

"They want to know who was drawing on Charlie's social security deposits from his bank account. Who approved the checks Charlie supposedly signed and we cashed after he was dead? Did the Home have any program to monitor residents' well-being, most of whom were recipients of one or another federal program where funds went to the care providers?" wailed Jane. "They are painting him as a criminal."

"Or an idiot," whispered one of the Geezers.

"They say he's facing a fifteen-year prison sentence if he can't come up with some answers," cried a despondent Jane as I gave her a tissue.

After two hours, the agents left the building, smug looks on their faces. Leroy went into Harvey's office and spent fifteen or twenty minutes before emerging with Harvey. Leroy saw us in the study and motioned for us to join them.

"You've all witnessed the morning events. I believe Jane has given you a description, perhaps a bit hysterically, of what is going on. I think it best, and Harvey agrees," he said as he nudged Havey's shoulder to get a head nod, "that you know the actual details before rumors start."

"As you know, it is a federal offense to cash the social security checks of the deceased. Charlie had direct deposit. The FBI is suggesting *La Petit Refuge* is culpable for not timely notifying the bank of Charlie's death, and before you say Harvey didn't know, they are suggesting he is guilty of not knowing the status of his charges."

At this point, I had to add my two cents. "Given we are not 'his charges,' we are all free to come and go at will and have no obligation to inform the house of our movements, even though you have asked us to. That is a totally bogus charge, a charge merely to intimidate."

Harvey looks up with some hope in his eyes, and I add, "Get a good lawyer."

# 10  The Emerald Mile

Meanwhile, just off "The Emerald Mile," in Younkers, Eddie Boyle was talking with his two younger brothers Hugh and Gavin. "I saw the old man last month. He's adamant. He won't move out of that retirement home. I told him we could get him better care up here. His response '*I bought the damn place, and I'm damn well going to stay here.*'"

"He's afraid he's still on the FBI's wanted list. I told him once, if not a dozen times, the statute of limitations has run on those federal racketeering charges," said Gavin.

"Getting back to business," Eddie said; "where are the two shipments?"

"Containers are being offloaded at New Jersey's Newark-Elizabeth Port as we speak," responded Gavin. I still think it's a hair-brained idea to sell counterfeit sports gear. If the customer inspector finds 'Made in America' labels, the entire shipment will be confiscated.

"Not to worry, the inspector's been paid off."

"I still don't like it," said Gavin. "Gramps made the family money the good old-fashioned way -- bootleg whiskey. We are just hawking t-shirts."

"And if you emblazon them with *New York Giants,* you can sell them for a hundred times their cost.

"Same with *Green Bay Packers, Washington Commanders,* or *San Fransico 49s*; fans will buy anything, even the crap we import," added Hugh.

"What about the *Mets*?" asked Gavin.

The other two looked at him. "They can't even give away tickets to their home games," said a chuckling Eddie.

If all goes as planned, the shipment should be broken down and moved to our mail-order outlets by the end of the week.

"Gavin, I want you to take a truckload down to Florida. I have a new buyer in Miami. I promised him a shipment this month. And then go to West Palm Beach and see Dad. Maybe you can get him to see reason. He's always listened to you."

"Hugh, how have you handled the incursions into our territory by the Puerto Ricans? I told you I want those *spics* gone," said Eddie.

"We found one spying on Dad; that's another reason to get him to move. Butch dealt with him. I don't think *Daidi* ever knew, But one of the residents, a retired cop, an old geezer with apparent dementia, stumbled across the aftermath of Butch's work. Should we tell Butch to take care of him?" asked Hugh.

Mulling it over, Eddie said, "No. That will just attract more attention."

# 11 The Shipment

"I still think Eddie has lost it," Gavin was saying as he and Hugh pulled into the container lot. "What container numbers are we looking for?"

"HLXU2008419 and TLLU5146210," said Hugh. "The guard at the gate said the attendant was back here in lane 23B. Is that him up there?"

Approaching the attendant, Gavin hands him the documents for the container and asks where they are. The attendant quickly scans the paperwork and then more slowly reads through it. "These two containers were picked up early this morning," he says.

"BY WHO!! yells Gavin.

"I don't know. They had the proper paperwork. I think they were speaking Spanish," said the attendant, who was now becoming more frightened as he saw Gavin's shoulder holster.

"Eddie's going to be pissed." Turning to the attendant, Hugh asks if there are security cameras?"

"Yes."

"I want a copy of this morning's recording."

"I can't give you that," said the attendant.

Taking out a large clasp knife, Gavin says, "I'm going to start cutting off your fingers," as Hugh grabs his arm, "until I get the recording – do you understand?"

"Y, y y yes the attendant stutters. They're back in my office."

Leaving the container lot with the video recording, "It was those spics," utters Gavin. "I recognized the guy with the paperwork."

Eddie took the news rather calmly, all things considered. "This is war, "he said, "call the boys in, all of them."

"Even the ones running numbers? Hugh asks.

"All of them."

By three that afternoon, seven of the Kinahan Cartel bosses were seated around the conference table in Eddie Boyle's office. The remaining two were enjoying the hospitality of the NYPD.

"I want my shipment back," said Eddie. "Bring me their leader. If there is resistance, shoot them."

Over the next several days, bodies were piling up in Spanish Harlem. The police looked on with some indifference -- *looks like another mob war* was the sentiment.

Finally, Ernesto Rodriguez, head of the Puerto Rican syndicate, was found and brought to a back room on the Emerald Mile.

"Ernesto, good of you to stop in," said Eddie. "I don't believe we've had the pleasure before. Now, before this gets messy, I want my containers back and the heads of these two punks," Eddie said as he showed Rodriguez a photo taken from the video. "Who took them, and where are my containers?"

"Go f ……. yourself said, Rodriguez."

"Now, perhaps you have heard of me, Eddie 'the blade' Boyle is my old nickname," Eddie said as he picked up a large bowie knife. "Thank you. I wanted an excuse to practice my old hobby." Turning to the two large men on either side of the reluctant Rodriguez, "Take his left shoe off and hold his leg on the table."

With a quick stroke, a toe was severed; Rodriguez was screaming, and Eddie was poking the tip of his knife into Rodriguez's big toe.

"Again," Eddie said, pointing to the photo. "who took them, and where are my containers? I will carve all the way up your leg to your balls. You're going to talk, so save yourself some agony."

Grimacing, Rodriguez spit out an address.

"If there is nothing there, I'll carve you like a Christmas goose," said Eddie.

That night, Gavin called in. "We found the containers; one is empty. The men here are leaking like sieves; we should be able to trace the merchandise."

"Good." Turning to Hugh, "Bring Rodriguez back in."

"Ernesto, we found my containers. Thank you. I'll have my boys take you back to Spanish Harlem."

# 12   Tienda de Deportes

By now, most of Eddie's merchandise was in four states.   One U-Hall was on I-95 headed to Miami.   Clementi Moreno, the driver, was one of the men featured in the video recording.   His destination was a large sporting goods store, *Tienda de Deportes*[2], popular with the Cuban community.   And then well-deserved time on the beach watching bikinis.

Days later, Butch was watching his car crew waxing one of the Cadillacs.   "I want to see my reflection, good enough to shave with," he joked with Juan.

Juan, a Cuban refugee, had been with the old man since the old man came to Florida a decade ago.   Juan was Boyel's driver and general gofer.

"Where did you get that Mets t-shirt?" asked Butch; "the colors are running down your arm."

---

[2] Sports Store

"My son got it from *Tienda de Deportes*; they just got a shipment of cheap football shirts. They are having a hard time giving them away."

Later that day, Butch recounted this conversation to Leim, the senior on-site man. "Hold that thought," Leim said as he pulled out his cell and hit the programmed number for Gavin. "Gavin, this is Leim. I got a story for you, I'll let Butch tell you."

After Butch recounted Juan's story about the t-shirt, Gavin said, "Hold tight, I'll get back to you."

Not more than ten minutes had passed, Leim's cell was chirping. "Leim, this is Eddie. Go to the store that's selling that crap and find out where it came from – today!"

"Yes boss., I'm on it."

Leim and Butch put on business suits and paid a visit to the *Tienda de Deporte's* buyer. Liliana, an attractive lady in her mid-30s, was at first reluctant to talk with the two until it was intimated that they were Feds tracking fake Chinese imports.

"You know it's a federal offense to sell Chinese knockoffs," said Leim. "You have several tables of cheap t-shirts for sale that were not made in America as their labels say. We would appreciate your help in tracking down the people who sold you this merchandise."

Liliana, now anxious, told the two about the young man who sold her the goods at a remarkably low price.

Butch showed her the photo lifted from the port's security tape, "Do you recognize either of these two people?"

Liliana took the photo and studied it for a moment, "The man on the right is the one who sold me the goods."

"Do you know where he is?"

"No, but he did say something about getting some time on the beach."

As the two men turned to leave, Liliana asked, "What should I do with the shirts?"

"Burn them, you don't want to associate the name of your store with that crap," said Leim.

Later that night, Leim reported the day's events to Gavin. "We want that man – dead – said Gavin. I'll send some people to help you search the beaches. Pick them up at the airport in the morning."

"What time will they be here," asked Butch.

"Gavin didn't say which flight; we'll meet them all."

The nine o'clock flight from JFK had seven of Gavin's men on it.

"Damn, we don't have room for all of them in the van," said Butch.

"Stuff them in; they can sit on each other's laps," was Leim's curt reply.

# 13  The Search

Leim had rented a motel room near the airport.  Everyone was directed to change into the beach clothes Gavin had told them to bring.  Leim and Butch also had a change of outfits handy.

When changed, Leim had them assemble, where he provided directions.  "Each of you will be dropped off along the beach, and you are to look for this man," he said as a copy of the print was passed to each.  "If you see him, DO NOT approach him; call me at the number on the back of the handout. Is that clear?"

"Yes," was the murmured reply.

"Do we go alone or in teams?" one asked.

"Since you are not to confront him, you will be by yourself. I want to cover as much of the beach as possible," said Leim. "Any more questions?"

Starting at the south end of Ocean Drive, one man was dropped off about every two miles along the beach up to Hollywood.

It was a long, hot day.  Late that afternoon, Leim's phone chirps.

"I got him!"

"Where are you," said an excited Leim.

"Just a little north of mile marker four, about halfway between the two lifeguard stands."

"Stay with him; we're on our way."

Leim and Butch were parked at mile marker ten, and within minutes, Butch was dropping Leim off at the beach.

Leim was wearing blue swim trunks, a Jets baseball cap, wraparound sunglasses, and carrying a beach bag.

He quickly located his scout – and his target.

He provided last-minute instructions to the scout, pulled out a palm-size .22 derringer, and wrapped it and his hand in a red beach towel.  As Leim walked up behind the man snoozing on the beach, the scout took the air horn he was given and began running along the beach, blasting the horn.  Leim quickly kneeled, wrapped the end of the towel around his target's head, and shot him in the base of the skull.  The towel muffled the shot as any would be witness focused on the nut with the air horn.

Leim left his victim's head cradled in the towel so fellow beachgoers would think the man was using the towel as a pillow.  It wasn't until later that one of the beach lifeguards became concerned about the body that had not moved for the last few hours.

# 14  Spanish Harlem

Ernesto Rodriguez slammed the Miami Herald down on the table. It was open to an article on page seven. This action caused him severe pain in his left foot.

> Is New York sending mob violence to Florida? It was only a few months ago that a body, partially eaten by an alligator, a member of NYC's Puerto Rican crime family, was pulled from a Palm Beach canal. Yesterday, lifeguards on a Miami beach found the body of another member of this crime family - lying on the beach as if sleeping with a bullet in the back of his head.

Who are they talking about, Rafael? Who are the dead bodies?

Rafael Machado, one of Ernesto's lieutenants, replied, "The first was Emilio Rodriguez. Several months ago, I sent him to Florida to find 'old man' Boyle, Eddie Boyle's father. He disappeared a few months ago. The guy on the beach was

Clementi Moreno. Last week he took a truckload of that sports crap to Florida to sell," *when you were getting your pedicure,* Rafael thought to himself.

"And did Emilio have any luck in finding Boyel?" asked Ernesto.

"Not that we know of; he never reported back."

"That's a shame. I want you to find that SOB. I can't get his son; too many *micks* protecting him in Yonkers, but if I can find his father ......".

"I'll send Diego and his crew to continue the search," said Rafael

*\*\*\**

Rafael was talking with Diego and his crew, three young Latinos who called themselves the *'tres mosqueteros'* with Diego playing the role of d'Artagnan.

"The boss wants you to find Eddie Boyel's father. He's somewhere in Florida, probably in the Miami area." Adding an encouraging thought, Diego ended with, "Do you remember Emilio Rodriguez? I sent him down there earlier this year ...... his body, half eaten by alligators, was found in Palm Beach."

# 15  The White Box Truck

Meanwhile, across town in Younker, Eddie is giving Gavin his marching orders. "I want you to take a truckload of that sportswear we recovered down to my new buyer in Florida, then go see what Leim is up to. And take a couple of the boys with you; they deserve some time on the beach."

Three of Eddie's boys are headed south that Thursday in a white box truck. Sharing the driving, they were entering Dade county eighteen hours later.

"Let's stop at a motel," said Tito. "Eddie's contact won't be at the store tonight. There's a Motel 6 just ahead; we can get two rooms."

"No," said Gavin; the contact just texted me; he's waiting for us now.

Following the directions the contact provided, Gavin pulls the truck up to the loading dock of *Tienda de Deportes*. The contact is there and directs Gavin and his men where to put the cargo.

"You made good time from New York," the contact says when the loading dock door bursts open and a pissed-off Latina starts yelling.

"Manwell, what the hell are you doing?"

"Liliana, I got a good deal on some sportswear, pennies on the dollar," Manwell replies in an uncertain voice.

"The Feds were here three days ago and directed me to burn that load of knockoffs I bought and threatened me with jail time."

Turning to Gavin, "Get this crap off my loading dock before I call the Feds!!"

Back in her office, Liliana searched through her desk to find the number Agent Boyle had left with her.

"Agent Boyle, this is Liliana ... yes, from *Tienda de Deportes.* I just wanted to let you know there was a group here, just ten minutes ago, trying to sell us some more of that Chinese crap. There were three of them in a white box truck. The truck had New York plates.... no, I didn't get the number. ... Yes, I'll let you know if I see them again. Goodbye."

At *La Petit Refuge,* as Leim is putting his cell away, he comments to Butch, "That was that hot Latina from *Tienda de Deportes.* She thinks I'm a Fed; someone is trying to sell her more Chinese knockoffs."

Within the hour a white box truck pulls into the alley behind the *Refuge*. As Gavin begins to tell Leim of the evening events, Gavin and Butch break out laughing.

"What's so funny?" yells a steamed Gavin.

Leim tells Gavin of the call he just received from Liliana and why she thinks he is an FBI agent.

"Christ, why didn't someone tell me? Does Eddie know?"

Sitting around later that night, after a few beers, "I need to kill that bitch," says Gavin, "she can identify me."

"No, I'll take care of it," said Liem, "just avoid Miami for the next few days."

Three days late, Liem calls Liliana. "I just wanted you to know," he says, "that those guys trying to sell you the knockoffs last week are dead. They were at Amos's Sports store on Auburn Avenue in Atlanta when one of the clerks, unpacking the merchandise, noticed a misspelling. Atlanta was spelled 'Atlante' on the Atlanta Braves t-shirts. Local fans didn't take that well, and a riot ensued. The truck was burned, and, well, it didn't turn out well for your friends."

Turning to Gavin, give it a few days, and your face will be dead to her.

# 16  Paddy's Revenge

The Geezer's morning get-together was breaking up when I noticed T and Leroy in an animated discussion. Curious and never one to mind my own business, I wandered over to the front reception desk. T was saying, "You need to tell Bains about these people."

Intruding, I asked, "What people?"

"There some people, Puerto Ricans I think, asking about an old white dude that may live somewhere around here. He disappeared long time ago. They have a message to deliver."

"I ain't telling Harvey nothing," said Leroy. "You best be getting back out there to find your next rumor."

After T left, I reminded Leroy of the body found in the canal a couple of months ago, shortly after Betty reported a body on the third floor. "He was Puerto Rican as I remember."

"Okay, I'll pass it on to Harvey. Perhaps the people in the back should be told," said a reluctant Leroy. "I just don't want to get in the middle of this shit."

Going up to my room, it hit me, 'Bloody' Boyel. In the mid-60s, there was a blood feud between the Puerto Rican syndicate and the Irish mob. Sean 'Bloody' Boyel headed the latter. As I recall the events from over five decades ago, the Connecticut Valley was a battleground. It started in Springfield when a catholic priest, with mostly Irish parishioners in the city's 'south end,' refused to say mass for The Lady of Guadalupe on St. Paddy's Day. The people requesting the mass were Puerto Ricans from the 'north end.' The Saint Patrick's Day parade was disrupted by masked thugs, resulting in the hospitalization of many participants, including the priest. It was never proven who the masked thugs were, but it was widely believed they were Puerto Rican gang members.

Sean Boyle was the Irish mob's 'godfather.' Based in NYC, he held sway over the Irish mob from Atlantic City to Boston and all points in between. With his catholic upbringing, he took the attack on an Irish priest personally.

Sean took some of his 'boys,' went to Springfield, and, with local help, decimated the local branch of the Puerto Rican syndicate. There were at least a dozen bodies. Mercy Hospital's ER was overwhelmed with casualties, mostly knife and blunt force trauma, the overflow being sent to Springfield General. It is rumored Sean took part; he personally conducted the execution of three of the Puerto Rican leaders. That was when he earned the nickname *'Bloody' Boyle*. The local paper, the Springfield Union, ran headlines for days, calling it *Paddy's Revenge*.

Some of the bloodletting flowed down the Connecticut Valley to Hartford county, where two more bodies were found, both small-time Puerto Rican hoods.

As I got to my room, my mind flashed back to that wizened old man I saw at the *Andrew Sister's Look-Alikes* performance. Could he be 'Bloody' Boyle?

Pulling out an old address book, I dug out the information number for the Hartford Police Department.

"Can I speak with Jim Miller?" I asked the operator. Jim was just coming on the force when I retired. I was his mentor for his first year. The last I heard of him was of his promotion to Commander of the Robbery Division.

"Jim, JB here. You still keeping Hartford safe?" ... "No, I'm not calling to see how your Hartford Eagles are doing." As I recall, Jim was a big baseball fan and had played for the Eagles before joining the police force.

After a little more banter, I got to the point. "Do you remember the 1963 Paddy's Revenge murders in Springfield and the overflow to Hartford? ... Ya, I guess that was before your time; you were probably in grade school. When I left, it was an open FBI case and probably still is. As I recall, there was a nationwide manhunt for Sean Boyle. He was never caught. I need a favor. Could you go to the cold case files and get me a copy of Boyel's wanted poster?" ... "Thanks, text it to me. I'll get someone here to help me download it."

# 17  Bloody Boyle

Sometime during the night, Jim texted me the poster. The next morning, looking at my cell, '*How the hell do I get into this attachment?*' was my first thought.

I got dressed and went to find Leroy. The receptionist's desk was unmanned. Glancing at the clock on the wall, I saw that it was only 6:27. Leroy was not normally in until seven. Great. I get coffee and find my usual seat in 'Geezer's Hall' -- no one is there. Picking up an old paper, I idly start paging through it. Jimmy Abdow's article in the Miami Harold from last week caught my attention.

> Is New York sending mob violence to Florida? It was only a few months ago that a body, partially eaten by an alligator, a member of NYC's Puerto Rican crime family, was pulled from a Palm Beach canal. Yesterday, lifeguards on a Miami beach found the body of another member of this crime family - lying on the beach as if sleeping with a bullet in the back of his head.

My mind flips back to T's comments yesterday '*There some people, Puerto Ricans I think, asking about an old white dude that may live somewhere around here. He disappeared long time ago. They have a message to deliver.*' Bloody Boyel was my first thought this morning.

Leroy is a few minutes early and I'm at his desk before he is settled in. "Leroy, can you get an attachment off my phone?"

"Sure. Give me a minute; let me put this stuff away." A moment later, "Okay, what ya got?" he asks.

I take my phone and show him Jim's text message.

"Not a problem; let me send it to the printer." Somehow, Leroy connects my cell to the printer, and lo and behold, it comes to life, spitting out a page.

Leroy takes the page and, after looking at it, becomes a shade lighter. He thrust it to me and said in an excited voice, "I ain't seen this, and it's best you never have either!"

I take the printout, and if I didn't know better, it's a wanted poster for Eddie Boyle.

"This looks just like the photo of Eddie Boyle we took a few weeks ago," I say, "yet it's a wanted poster for Sean Boyle from the 1960s."

'*Is Eddie Sean's son?*' I ask myself since Leroy is now on the other side of the lobby, trying to ignore me.

\*\*\*

A taxi ride takes me to the Palm Beach Police Headquarters building. "I'm looking for Detective Randy Alistair," I tell the sergeant at the front desk.

Looking up, he sees an old man with a walker, "Have a seat over there gramps," he says, pointing to a row of seats by the wall. "I'll call upstairs to see if he is in."

Five minutes later, Randy comes down the stairs, "JB, what are you doing here? Let's go to my office."

Looking at my walker, he takes me to the elevator. Once in his office, he offered me coffee, which was declined, and then "What's up?"

I take out Sean Boyle's wanted poster and lay it on his desk, "I'm claiming the reward," I say. "I could take this to the FBI, but you being a friend, I'll let you get the credit for his capture."

I then spend the next fifteen minutes laying out my case. I take the story back to 1963, Paddy's Revenge, and how Sean Boyle earned the nickname Bloody Boyle.

"There will probably be bodies at the retirement home in the next few days," I say as I recount T's words. "The Puerto Ricans have been looking for Bloody Boyle for the past five decades. They are closing in."

"Pete told me yesterday, he's the guy who took Eddie's picture, that he's spotted at least three more men, possibly gunmen, at the home's back entrance as well as a box truck."

"Tell me what you know about the body the Miami police found on the beach last week. Who whacked him?" I asked.

"Randy, I suggest the PBPD up its game in the *La Petit Refuge* neighborhood."

"Sit tight," he said as he got up and went to the Captain's office. I could see their heads bobbing up and down, occasionally looking over at me. The Captain made a phone call.

Ten minutes later, Randy called me into the Captain's office. "Randy tells me you are a former homicide detective. You have a premonition of a pending murder spree in West Palm Beach," said the Captain. "I just called my Dad; he's the former Miami chief of police. He now lives at *The Villages* and plays bridge weekly with other retired cops. One is the former Hartford chief of police, Bill Goodman. You should know him. I asked Dad to check with Goodman about you. He tracked Bill down at the pickleball court. Bill's reply, you are a credible officer, and I would be wise to listen to you."

"Randy, I want patrols doubled in the vicinity of the *La Petit Refuge* neighborhood. Put some feelers out and see what tidbits you can pick up. In the meantime, I'm going to coordinate with the FBI."

# 18 The Prelude

"Harvey's FBI friends are back," said Gerald, looking into the lobby.

"I'll give you even odds Harvey has a panic attack in the next five minutes," joked Sammy as the agents were ushered into Harvey's office.

It's not long before the agents emerge and storm out of the building. Jane is next out of the office, rushes over to the receptionist's desk, and is franticly flaying her arms, trying to get Leroy to do something.

Taking charge, Gerald quickly intervenes between the two, exchanges a few words with Leroy, and leads Jane into the sitting room.

"Okay Jane, tell us what is going on while Leroy tracks down one of the health aide's to help Harvey."

Taking a deep breath, Jane looks around, "The FBI wants a list of all our residents."

"That's not so terrible, is it?" I said.

"Then they want Harvey to assemble them all in the lobby for questioning – as they search the building."

"Then, I'm ever so proud of Harvey; he stood up and told them to get out, telling them to '*get a warrant or kiss his ass.*'" When they left, Harvey collapsed. That's when I went to Leroy asking for help."

At that moment, I thought it best not to mention yesterday's visit to the PBPD. The Captain clearly followed through with his promise to contact the FBI. I hopefully assumed he also increased police patrols in the area.

Two days later, one of the Rufuge's maintenance men was hospitalized. He claimed two Hispanics jumped him and demanded information on the home's residents. When he resisted, they beat him, eventually getting the information they wanted. They were most interested in the recluse living in the south wing's first floor.

     \*\*\*

Back in Spanish Harlem, "That was Diego," said Ernesto as he severed the connection on his cell. "They found Bloody Boyle. He's living in a retirement home, *La Petit Refuge of Boynton Beach.*"

"There appear to be five or six Irish mob boys there. Rafael, let's make this a twofer. We'll take out Bloody Boyle and his mick bodyguards."

"Diego has two men with him. You take four more, and let's put an end to these bastards. This may be enough to get Eddie Boyle off the Emerald Mile, and we'll get him to."

"You know this will be a declaration of war," said Diego.

"No, Sean Boyle declared war on us in 1963 when he killed my father. I'm here to finish it," said Ernesto.

# 19   The Letdown

T's boys were reporting several young Hispanic men moving into the Boynton Beach area. They stood out from the geriatric crowd. He reported this to Leroy, who, in turn, told me, and I passed the information on to Randy. Based on this information, the PBPD posted several squad cars in the area.

***

On that fateful day in September, the Puerto Ricans staged their seven men two blocks from La Petit Refuge, just behind Publix. Their plan was to hit the rear of the Refuge at daylight, breaching the south wing's rear door. They figured the door would be reinforced, so they planned to blow it off its hinges. They would kill everyone they found. Caddies were to be torched. The escape path would be the way they came, with the two SUVs parked behind Publix. Once they got on I-95, they'd be home free.

"Remember, the boss wants a video of Boyle being shot," said Rafael. "Diego, you are our videographer. Record everything, keep the boss happy."

Unbeknownst to both the Puerto Ricans and the Palm Beach Police, the FBI staged their strike force a mile down Rt. 1, preparing for an early morning raid on La Petit Refuge to arrest Sean 'Bloody' Boyle, hopefully before many of the residents were up. Their plan was to sweep in and surround the building while their main force focused on the south wing's first floor.

***

Sean Boyle screwed up these plans. He died peacefully in his sleep just after midnight. His live in hospice nurse promptly reported the death to the county coroner's office. The coroner's practice was to remove bodies as quickly as possible to avoid upsetting residents. The 'meat' wagon was at La Petit Refuge by 2 a.m. The night porter let them in with their gurney. The coroner's night assistant talked with the nurse and filled out the required papers. By three, Sean was headed to the *Everlasting Peace Funeral Home.* The death would not be reported to the police until eight that morning. By four a.m., the night porter was snoozing once again in one of the lobby's overstuffed chairs.

At five a.m. sharp, black FBI SUVs quietly encircled La Petit Refuge. The lead agent, dressed in riot gear, scared the crap out of the night porter beating on the locked lobby door to be let in.

The FBI team secured the lobby with the main body breaking through the door to the apartment complex in the south wing. There were two shots fired, one by Gavin and the other by an FBI agent. Gavin's bullet hit the leading agent in the chest. That agent, wearing a bulletproof vest, went down. His only injury was a severe black and blue bruise on his chest. Gavin, on the other hand, was dead. The following agent's bullet caught Gavin mid-chest, penetrating his heart. Five others were taken into custody with no incidents.

As Butch was being led away, the lead agent asked where Sean 'Bloody' Boyle was. Butch looked at him and started laughing, "You stupid fool, you're a day late. He's dead."

***

An hour earlier, the Puerto Ricans started to make their move. They were coming in on foot, Rafael in the lead, when he saw the two black SUVs pull up in the back of the retirement home. Four men in tactical gear got out and took up defensive positions in the alley.

"Shit, what's the FBI doing here," he mutters to himself just as two gunshots ring out. Turning to his boys, "Let's get out of here."

As they scrambled back to the SUVs parked behind Publix, four PBPD vehicles boxed them in. Framed in the cruiser's spotlights, blinding them, they were ordered to raise their hands and face the wall. The police frisked each and put them in cuffs.

# 20  Debriefing

It wasn't until early afternoon that Randy was able to meet me at the Residence.  When he got there, the place was like an anthill that someone kicked.  The home's occupants were milling around in the lobby, hoping to get the latest morsel of news.  Leroy was forced to repeat what he knew of the night's events for each new arrival.

Harvey had the vapors.  Jane had him lying on the couch in his office.  And the Geezers had taken up their position in the study where they could monitor the lobby.

As Randy entered, I quickly got up and motioned for him to join us.  If the crowd caught him, we'd be in the dark for hours.  Fortunately, he saw me and joined us.

Sitting down, my first question was, "What the hell happened last night?"

Looking around the table, looking at us, he said with a chuckle, "Your police department looking out for you."

"Okay, here is what happened," he said.

"Just after midnight, Sean Boyle, your neighbor in the south wing, expired. The coroner had the body out of here by three. Sean is now at the *Everlasting Peace Funeral Home,* probably having a good laugh."

"Based on JB's gut feeling, which my Captain shared with the FBI, the FBI went after Sean 'Bloody' Boyle. He's been on their wanted list for the last fifty years. Not knowing Boyle was dead, the FBI executed their raid to arrest him at five this morning. There was some gunfire, one of Boyle's foot soldiers was killed, and several were arrested."

"Concurrent with that fiasco, the Puerto Rican syndicate had a hit team in motion to take out 'Bloody' Boyle. Based on the information Leroy got from T and his boys, we were tracking them."

"The Puerto Rican/Irish vendetta goes back to the '60s. JB here can tell you the details. Anyway, the FBI's action forced them to cancel their plans to kill Boyle. As they were making their getaway, the police nabbed them. Seven are now in custody. Unfortunately, they will be back on the street by the end of the day. They've done nothing that we can charge them with."

"My Captain is livid that the FBI didn't notify him of their pending raid. Today's newspaper article will have us all looking like the Keystone Cops, tripping over each other in the dark. They were interviewing Captain Hardy when I left to come here."

"He is also ripped at the county coroner's office. He wants all natural deaths reported to the police in real-time, not the next morning."

Looking at Randy I say, "Now that I found Boyle for you, when do I get the reward? Ten thousand dollars, I believe."

Randy looks at me and laughs. "I'm glad you have a sense of humor; I needed that. You can take up the reward with the Feds – good luck."

# 21 Keystone Cop Tour

Harvey had mostly recovered by the following week and was able to manage the monthly community meeting. He opens with, "As you have all heard, we had some excitement here last week. The FBI has interviewed most of you. If you know anything about Mr. Boyle, please share it with them."

"The FBI was most impressed with the photos Pete Miller took. The box truck found in the alley contained knockoff sports gear. The two gentlemen associated with the truck, identified in Pete's photos, are being held on minor import violations but are expected to be released by the end of the week. They have a good New York lawyer. All other occupants of Mr. Boyle's apparent complex are gone.

"Jane and I hope to get the *La Petit Refuge* back to the happy community we were before the recent disruptions. Leroy has several social outings scheduled over the next few weeks that I hope many of you will take advantage of."

"Does that include the La Bumba Nightclub?" shouted out Tony.

A little flustered, Harvey responded, "Wholesome outings!"

"Harvey is a frequent customer," comments one of the older Geezers to no one in particular.

"No, he's not," sputters Jane as many of the residents suppress nervous laughter.

As the crowd, the fifteen or so residents, break up, Leroy comes over to our table and takes the empty seat. "The next few weeks will be interesting," he says. "It was the Boyle group, the owners, who was telling Harvey what to do. He's going to be lost."

\*\*\*

Life went on pretty much as normal for the next few weeks. Harvey made occasional appearances to cheer up the inmates; Jane would appear shortly thereafter to explain what Harvey meant. And Leroy would tell us all to disregard and get on with our day.

T and his boys continued looking out for us, but they now had a new side gig, conducting tours of the 'Boyle Hideout,' five dollars a head. To reward the gang for their help, Leroy gave T a key to the backdoor. The tour that T called *Florida's Keystone Cops* went something like this:

Entering the alley from Publix's parking lot, T would point out where the Puerto Ricans were staging their assault. Entering the south wing's ground floor, the tour of Boyle's apartment complex would end in his bedroom, T pointing out the bed in which Boyle died.

At this point, T would go into great detail describing how the FBI and the Puerto Ricans were planning, oblivious to each other, simultaneous assaults on Boyle's hideout, and then Bloody Boyle snookered both of them by peacefully dying in his sleep hours earlier.

Next, moving to the interior of the apartment, T would point out the chalk body outline of where Gavin's body fell during his gun battle with the Feds. Exiting the apartment the way the tour had begun, T described how the Puerto Ricans had run when they heard the gunshots and fled, into the arms of the police.

Later, when Jane told Harvey about the tour, he exploded.

"Leroy, he yelled as he burst into the lobby, "What's this I hear about T's *Florida's Keystone Cops* tour. It's making *La Petit Refuge* a joke! At yesterday's retirement home managers quarterly meeting, I noticed people pointing at me and laughing."

"It wasn't because of T's tour," whispered one of the Geezers" standing at Leroy's desk.

"What was that?" sputtered Harvey.

"Just commenting on T's capitalist spirit; do you know he's made several hundred dollars? Now, at five dollars a head, half of Boynton Beach must have taken the tour."

As Harvey's face turns a shade of red, and he retreats to his office, Leroy says, "That wasn't nice, Pete. Poking the poor guys when he's already down."

# 22  Evection Threat

At the community meeting a few months after the Boyle incident, Harvey dropped some disturbing news on us.

"Mr. Boyle owned *La Petit Refuge*. I don't know who the new owner will be. His son in New York? There is some talk that the property will be confiscated by the federal government as property gained from criminal activity. The property may be sold."

"I don't know if *La Petit Refuge* will be allowed to continue to operate as a retirement home," said Harvey. "Palm Beach County is noncommittal as to the renewal of the Home's license, given the uncertainty of ownership. Our future here is tenuous; you might start thinking about alternative living arrangements."

As residents broke into small groups to discuss their future, some with great animation, the Geezers convened in the study. "That was one hell of a speech Harvey gave," said Jeb. "Usually, he's wishy-washy, all over the place. But no, today he's clear, leaving residents in a state of near panic."

"It can't be as bleak as he painted it," said Gerald. "Collectively, we have over six hundred years of experience. What are some solutions?"

"Well, we could buy some surplus cargo containers and move into them," I said. After some groans, "Okay, that was a bad joke."

That evening, I called my niece. "Barb, a few weeks ago, I told you about the Keystone Cop episode down here. ... Yes, Harvey is back to his normal self; that's why I'm calling. Today he announced that the ownership of the *La Petit Refuge* is in question. Palm Beach County is noncommittal as to its renewal of the Home's license, given the uncertainty of ownership. And to quote Harvey from this morning, '*Our future here is tenuous; you might start thinking about alternative living arrangements.*' John has offered to take me in, but that arrangement would only last a few days, a week at the most before we got on each other's nerves. He and I will start looking at other retirement homes next week. ... No, I'm not moving to Virginia," and I added with a chuckle, "You have winter there."

Well, that call went better than I expected. I had visions of Barb launching a full-scale attack on Harvey and Palm Beach County.

Little did I know that directly after my call, Barb called her daughter. Wanda is a senior lawyer at the Department of Housing and Urban Development. She's never married. Her passion is fair and equitable housing. She's been the face of HUD in several recent legal disputes with local governments regarding housing for minorities and the elderly. Her adversaries dubbed her as '*that bitch on steroids.*' The last time I saw my great-niece was twenty or twenty-five years ago when she visited. The visit was just an afterthought; she was here for spring break. At the time, Wanda was in her third year of law school. She and her friends were on the beach when two drunk and rowdy groups of undergraduates from rival schools faced off. In the resulting riot, she and her friends were arrested and charged with disorderly conduct. That would not stand. Wanda got the charges dropped after a short and vocal court hearing, and then she sued the police department. She won. The court found in her favor and awarded her five thousand dollars as a settlement.

# 23  Wanda

When Barb called, Wanda was up to eyeballs in work. "Can you look into this asked her mother. Uncle Joe may be out on the street by the end of the month. He doesn't have the money to fight this. He's going to end up in some shelter."

"Things don't move that fast," said Wanda. "Let me look into it."

The next morning, Wanda had her legal assistant look up recent news coverage of *La Petit Refuge* in Palm Beach, Florida.

"This is an interesting case," said Pam, Wanda's assistant. "Apparently, *La Petit Refuge* was owned by Sean Boyle, one of the FBI's most wanted. He's now dead. It's most likely it was purchased with mob money fifteen years ago, but that will be hard, if not impossible, to prove. His son, Eddie Boyle, has petitioned the court for ownership. The elder Boyle had no will. And to add some spice to this mix, the County of Palm Beach wants to condemn the property under eminent domain. A cousin of one of the county Commissioners wants to build condos."

"How many seniors will be displaced?" asked Wanda.

"A hundred and forty-seven, and before you ask, the county does not have available comparable housing. Other retirement homes in the area are charging three and four times what these people are now paying."

"You're painting a bleak picture."

"I think this might fall under our charter of protection of senior housing, much like that case you had last year in Denver," said Pam.

"Are you looking for a trip to Florida," joked Wanda. "Find out which courts are handling these cases: the son's petition for ownership and the county's move to take the property by eminent domain. I'll contact Andrew over at the FBI to see what their thoughts are. I have one other case pending. Let me see where that is, and let's plan to get back to *La Petit Refuge* on Monday."

\*\*\*

"The Judge Wilson has been assigned the two cases," said Pam. "His courtroom is in the North County Courthouse.

"Okay," said Wanda. "Draft a request a 30-day stay request for both cases, and I'll file it with the court."

"What about the FBI?"

"Oh, Andrew said the FBI has no interest in the property. They can't connect Boyle's mob money with its purchase."

"That's not likely," said Pam.

"Well, more specifically, he said there is no paper trail connecting the two. Anyway, that's one player off the table."

***

Going after the second player, Boyle's son, Wanda decides on the direct approach.

Arriving at Teterboro Airport, Wanda flags a taxi, "562 McLean Ave, in Younkers," she tells the driver, a small Hispanic man. He nods. Crossing the George Washington Bridge he says, "You know that's on the Emerald Mile, home of the Irish mob."

"Yes, so?"

"There's a turf battle going on between the Irish and the Puerto Ricans. I'm Puerto Rican," the driver says. "If you are seen with me, you may become a target."

"In fifteen minutes, that may be the least of my problems," said Wanda. "I'm going into the lion's den to stir the pot. There's a fifty-dollar tip if you wait for me at the curb."

562 McLean Ave. is an apartment building. Eddie has two of his men in the building's lobby, making it sort of like his reception area.

"I'm here to see Mr. Boyle," said Wanda.

Now, Wanda is not an unattractive woman, and the two goons spend a moment ogling her before asking, "Ya got an appointment?"

"He'll see me," she said, flashing her government ID, "or would you prefer I bring a couple of the City's finest? Eddie won't like that!"

The brightest of the two had a quick conversation on his cell, "Mr. Boyle is on the fourth floor he said," pointing to the elevator.

The elevator opens onto a dimly lit hallway where another of Eddie's men is waiting, "This way, please."

Wanda's lead into a large, well-furnished, and brightly lit room. It's obvious a wall or two has been taken down to create this space. A man, Wanda assumes to be Eddie, is sitting behind a large antique walnut desk. He gets up and offers his hand, "What's an attractive lady like you looking for an old Irishman like me? Let's have a seat over here where we can talk and be comfortable. Lemm, get us some coffee, or would you prefer tea?

"Coffee is fine. Thank you, black."

As they settle in, Eddie asks, "Who are you, and why are you here?"

Wanda answers his question, finishing up with, "The retirement home, *La Petit Refuge,* your father owned in Palm Beach. I want you to drop your claim to it."

"Why should I do that?" asks Eddie.

"You have an import company. Department of Treasury is holding two of your men for selling imported goods not properly declared."

Eddie immediately says, "I'm not responsible for two of my people skylarking on the side."

"And I'm not saying you are. But I have a colleague, an old schoolmate, Jacob Richerdson, working at Treasury, who complains of being so overworked he can't join his old classmates for a night out. I don't want to overburden him. I'm reluctant to suggest to Jacob that he might want to do a quick dive into the Shamrock Import Co. Now if I were focused on maintaining the *La Petit Refuge* as a retirement home for seniors with modest resources – well, I probably wouldn't have the time to call him."

"That's blackmail," sputters Eddie.

"Yes, and the concept is probably foreign to you."

"Look, we both know *La Petit Refuge* has no real value to you," said Wanda, "when compared to what you might lose. If you go to court, I'll challenge you, and it will cost more than the property is worth in legal fees."

Mulling this over, "How do I know you won't call this Richardson character when you walk out of her?"

"You don't. And I don't know if you won't refile your claim for La Petit Refuge."

Mulling this over Eddie says, "Lady, you drive a hard began. Okay, I'll trust you, and I promise to keep my end."

As they stood, "It's been interesting dealing with you," said Eddie. "I can truthfully say that I don't want the pleasure again," he said as he escorted Wanda to the elevator.

# 23  Seminole Casino

As the Geezers were discussing their future, Rodger Wilkins, the Boynton Beach Commissioner, was in an inebriated state at the Seminole Casino in Brighton. The Brighton Reservation, just to the west of Lake Okeechobee, is an easy drive from Palm Beach. Rodger was a frequent customer, rules were loose, and he could always get a line of credit when his luck turned on him.

Rodger met his future wife at Florida State University. After their marriage, he discovered that his new brother-in-law, William Black-Snake, owned the Seminole construction company.

William preferred his nickname, 'Big Willie.' Over the years, Rodger steered several public works projects to Big Willie, always realizing a reasonable kickback.

Rodger's latest scheme was to get his hands on *La Petit Refuge*. Ownership of the property was up in the air; Boyle's son had not stepped forward to claim the property. Rodger was pressing to have the county take the property by eminent domain. He would then propose the development of a new high-end condo complex, arguing that this would expand the county's tax base. Big Willie's construction company was not large enough to manage this project, but Rodger would make sure it was a major subcontractor.

"Damn," Rodger mutters as the croupier raked in his last chips.

Turning to Big Willie, "I need another house marker for a thousand," says Rodger.

"Rodger, the table is already carrying over $20K of your markers. You are in over your head."

"Nonsense, I can feel the next spin of the wheel. It's my turn to win!"

Big Willie nods to the croupier who then passes Rodger ten one-hundred-dollar chips.

Rodger, with a full glass of house scotch in one hand, pushes all ten chips onto a bet for Red. The croupier spins the wheel, around it goes, and the ball settles on 28 Black. Rodger's chips are reclaimed by the House.

With a shit-eating grin on his face, Rodger is calling for another marker as Big Willie escorts him from the casino by the elbow.

"Rodger, you are in for over $20K on the roulette table. Chief Watkins tells me are underwater by over a hundred grand in his weekly poker game. He wants his money in the next thirty days. Or…"

"Is that a threat? And what's he going to do? Take me to court for losing a rigged game. The res is a sovereign nation; he has no standing in our courts."

"Rodger, you need to cover this debt, or it's going to get ugly. Mortgage your house to get the money."

"Ha, my wife would never agree. Besides, the house is already mortgaged."

"Tell the Chief that as soon as I can get the *La Petit Refuge* condemned, the money will be in the pipeline. I have a motion before Judge Wilson. The hearing will be this Tuesday. There is a hotshot lawyer from HUD seeking a delay. Billie Jackson, the county's attorney, will smoke her."

"For your sake, I hope so," said Big Willie. "I hear the Chief is grooming his gators for a meal."

# 24  Court

Wanda and Pam deplaned in Miami, midmorning. Wanda insisted that Pam restrict her luggage to one carry-on. They slipped through the Arrival Terminal, out to the curb, and flagged down the National Rental Car shuttle. "You get the rental," said Wanda. I want to review my notes. "I have an appointment with the court clerk at two. Get directions from the agent."

"The North County Courthouse is on PGA Boulevard," said Pam. It's about sixty miles north of the airport, just off I-95 - a sixty-minute drive? We pass *La Petit Refuge* on the way if you would like to see it."

"Okay, we have time; let's do a drive-by," agreed Wanda.

La Petit Refuge is on Federal Highway, just a few blocks from I-95. Turning south on Federal Highway, "There it is," said. Pam.

"Pull into the parking lot. God, this place looks just like the Raddison Inn I stayed at in Denver," Wanda said. After a few moments surveying the building and parking lot, Wanda said she had seen enough, "Let's go."

North County Courthouse was located on Campus Drive; the parking lot was full. The two ladies were greeted by a passing cloud dispersing Florida liquid sunshine.

"Damn, we don't have an umbrella," complained Wanda. "Look over there. That car is leaving."

The ladies made it into the building with minimal damage. Brushing off the droplets, Pam pointed down the hall, "North county Court Clerk, that way," she said, reading the building directory.

As they headed down the hall, "Wanda?" someone called out.

Turning, a middle-aged man quickly approached,

"Wanda Zych, I haven't seen you since we graduated law school. You may not remember me, Jack Riely."

"Jack, of course I remember you. You were on the debating team. We opposed each other a few times. What was the topic – 'police authority to search cars pulled over for traffic violations' or some such nonsense?"

"Something like that. I'm working for Judge Wilson. I saw a request the other day that caught my eye. It was from a HUD attorney, Wanda Zych, requesting a stay in his decision regarding Palm Beach's eminent domain request. I take it that was you."

"Yes. We have a court hearing on my request at eleven today."

"Let's go into my office, and I will update you on it."

As Pam and Wanda were settling onto the couch in Jack's office, his secretary came in offering coffee. The two ladies declined.

"The Boynton Beach Commissioner is in a tizzy over your stay motion," said Jack. "As I understand the issue, the county wants to condemn the *La Petit Refuge* to make way for more condos and, in the process, displace the residents. You want to keep the *La Petit Refuge* under a HUD program that supports the housing of disadvantaged seniors. Your argument is that as long as Palm Beach County receives HUD funding, they are obligated to provide housing for disadvantaged seniors and that the county does not have the facilities to house the hundred and fifty or so seniors who will be displaced. You are proposing that the county, assisted with HUD funding, keep the *La Petit Refuge*. as a retirement home."

"Yup, that pretty much sums it up," said Wanda.

"Rodger Wilkins, the Boynton Beach Commissioner, is a pain in the ass," said Jack. It's well known that it's his brother-in-law who wants the property. He's a big developer in this part of the state. The brother-in-law is a big campaign donor. Judge Wilson is one of the recipients."

\*\*\*

"Ms. Zych, tell me why I should delay my decision on Palm Beach's request to take the property in question under the eminent domain," said the judge.

"Palm Beach, as a recipient of HUD grants, is obligated to find suitable housing for the low-income and senior residents displaced by actions resulting from those grants."

"The county has no obligation to those people. They are private citizens and are responsible for themselves," said Mr. Jackson, the county's attorney.

"Your Honor, under HUD Reg. 301.2, sub-paragraph 2a, recipients of HUD grants for low-income housing are obligated to provide suitable housing for people displaced by actions resulting from the application of these grants," said Wanda. "Palm Beach County is proposing to condemn *La Petit Refuge*, a retirement home occupied by low-income senior residents to build a new condominium complex. As required by county code, a certain percentage of these units are required to be set aside as low-income and will use HUD funds in their construction. No accommodation is being made for the home's current occupants. This is a clear violation of HUD Reg. 301.2, sub-paragraph 2a. I am here today requesting that your decision on the county's eminent domain action be delayed until the county can demonstrate there is adequate housing for the displaced senior residents."

"Mr. Jackson, your response, please."

"Your Honor, this is clearly a ploy by Washington bureaucrats to meddle in local affairs."

"Palm Beach County is a recipient of HUD funds?" asked the judge.

"Yes, but …"

"Enough Mr. Jackson. I have the HUD regulations here, thanks to my clerk, Jack Riely. I will delay my ruling for thirty days, as Ms. Zych requested. In thirty days, I expect you to present to the court Palm Beach County's plan on how the evicted seniors will be housed."

With that, the judge brings his gavel down, BANG.

"Court adjourned," yells out the bailiff.

Walking out of the courtroom, Jack turns to Wanda, "I'd love to take you out tonight, but my wife and twin three-year-olds have other plans."

"You're married? with kids … quite a change from your carefree days in law school," said Wanda. "Thank you for your help."

# 25  Boynton Beach

We drove into the Retirement Home's parking lot for the second time today. I called Uncle Joe after we left the North County Courthouse to tell him I would be stopping in later that afternoon. He was curious as to why I was in Florida. "I will tell you all about it when I see you," I told him.

Walking into the lobby, we were greeted by a pleasant middle-aged man. "Hello, I'm Leroy," he said, introducing himself. "What can I do for you?"

"We're here to see Joseph Barszcz."

"He's in the study with some friends. I'll get him for you."

Leroy goes to the back of the lobby, where there is a room overlooking the lobby, paneled with windows behind which there are at least a half dozen pairs of eyes watching us. He returns with Uncle Joe.

"Wanda, this is a surprise," he said while giving me a bear hug.

"Leroy, this is my great-niece, Wanda Zych." As the introduction comes to an end, I ask my great-uncle. "Is there somewhere we can talk in private?"

As Joe looks around, Leroy pipes up; you can use Harvey's office; he and Jane are out.

"Wanda, you have me worried. Is your Mother okay?"

"Yes, she's fine. She doesn't even know that I'm down here. But you are the reason for my visit."

My niece then spent the next fifteen minutes telling me why she was here, what she had been up to, and what was going to happen. I was spellbound.

"You can do that?" was all I could get out.

"Yes, I've already started. I have an appointment with the County Mayor tomorrow at eleven. A Mister Hugh Riddell, I believe. I stopped here first to see you but also, I'm hoping, to get background information on the Retirement Home."

That group of men you were with, can we talk with them?" Wanda asked.

I led the two ladies into the study. "This is Wanda, my great-niece. She's an attorney with HUD. She is focused on seniors. In other words, she's here to help."

"Where is her briefcase?" Gerald asked with a grin.

Ignoring him, I went on, "These are the Geezers; they can answer all your questions."

Wanda spent the next half hour going over most of what she had told me earlier. It took longer because there were more questions.

Wanda then asked a series of questions. How well is *La Petit Refuge* managed? Are there any maintenance issues? How is the staffing? Is it adequate? Who is the manager?

Some minor issues surfaced, but for the most part, the answers were well received.

"And the manager?" repeated Wanda.

"That would be Harvey Bains," said Gerald. "He's a competent manager, in fact quite good. But he often comes across as a twit. He has no people skills. His admin assistant, Jane, often has to cover for him."

"Okay, one last question," said Wanda. "Do you think Mr. Bains would be a responsible manager if the *La Petit Refuge* was independent of an owner, let's say, operating as a ward of the government?"

The Geezers sat and looked at each other. Finally, Pete spoke up, "Yes," and collectively, the group nodded their heads in agreement.

Leroy, who had been listening in at the door, said, "Harvey and Jane are back."

"I need to speak with Bains," said Wanda.

We walked across the lobby; by we, I mean Wanda and Pam, myself, and Gerald. Leroy knocked on Harvey's office doorframe; the door was already open, "Boss, there are some folks from HUD here to see you." With Leroy's emphasis on 'HUD,' one could see Harvey's face blanch.

We crowded into Harvey's office, with Leroy scaring up a couple of chairs so everyone could sit.

By the time Gerald finished with his summery, color had returned to Harvey's face.

"If I understand Gerald correctly, you are here to stop the county's action to close *La Petit Refuge*," said Harvey."

# 26  The Mayor

Palm Beach Government Center is on the northside of the county, on South Olive Avenue. Traffic was light, so we arrived for the eleven a.m. meeting with time to spare. Wanda and Pam were waiting for us in the lobby's coffee shop. Wanda asked Harvey to meet her there and to bring Gerald. I tagged along, having nothing better to do. And who knows, someone might buy me lunch.

The building directory placed the county Executive's office on the 7th floor. The lobby of the office provided an excellent view of the intercoastal waterway and an upscale marina.

"Do you have an appointment," asked a perky receptionist.

"Yes, with Hugh Riddell at eleven, the County Mayor," answered Wanda.

"Yes, here it is, but it was for only two; who are the other three?" asked Ms. Perky.

"Interested parties – and the Mayor's constituents.," responded Wanda.

With a somewhat condescending voice, she said, "Mayor Riddell will meet with you in conference room three, down the hall on the left."

We weren't the first there. Rodger Wilkins, the Boynton Beach Commissioner, and the county lawyer, Billie Jackson, were there. I think we interrupted what appeared to me to be a conspiratorial discussion.

"Ms. Zych, it's a pleasure to see you again," said the lawyer. "I hope we will be able to come to an amenable agreement today after yesterday's misguided ruling by Judge Wilson."

Before Wanda could reply, Mayor Riddell and his aide entered the room. "It is so nice everyone is here on time; I have a midday commitment I can't miss. Now, Ms. Zych, can you tell me why we are here today?"

Not to be put off her stride, "We're here to prevent Palm Beach County from displacing 147 senior residents from their home at *La Petit Refuge*. Mr. Wilkins is proposing to condemn *La Petit Refuge* and take the property by eminent domain. Under county ordinances, the high-end condominium proposed for the site requires that 10 percent of the units be set aside for low-income housing. His plan proposes the use of HUD funding for these units. This is in addition to the county's use of other HUD grants. Mr. Wilkins proposed action requires the county to provide comparable housing for the displaced seniors, housing which the county does not have. Neglect in doing so would put Palm Beach County in violation of HUD Reg. 301.2, sub-paragraph 2a."

"Mr. Wilkins, any comments?" asked the Mayor.

"Mayor Riddell, Ms. Zych, respectfully, is blowing smoke, as Mr. Jackson will explain."

"Your Honor, this is clearly a ploy by Washington bureaucrats to meddle in local affairs. If we stand our ground, Ms. Zych will have to take us to court – that's not going to happen. If she does, the case will drag on for years."

"Your Honor, you are clearly getting bad advice here," said Wanda. "I suggest you talk to your counterpart in Boulder, Colorado. Last year, I brought a similar case to the Federal District Court of Colorado. It cost Bolder fifty million dollars."

"Scare tactics," sputtered Billie Jackson.

"To continue the 'scare,' Palm Beach County is earmarked to receive a five-hundred-million-dollar HUD grant. If you intend to violate Reg. 301.2, sub-paragraph 2a, I will have to recommend to the Secretary of HUD to cancel this grant."

"You can't do that!" said an obviously panicked county attorney.

"That's my job," said Wanda, looking directly at him.

"Your Honor, if I'm not mistaken, you are running to be reelected in next year's elections; instead of putting senior citizens into homeless shelters, you could be using HUD grants to address the needs of the homeless in Palm Beach County."

"I think we could have a win-win here," said Wanda.

The Mayor's aide pulled the Mayor aside and spent five minutes in a side discussion with him.

When they emerged, the Mayor said, "Have Mr. Baines coordinate with my aide. Rodger, tell your brother-in-law to get stuffed; he's not getting the property."

# 27  Six Months Later

"Barb, you're fussing over me too much." I had just returned to *La Petit Refuge* after a three-day stay in the hospital. It was last week that I collapsed and Leroy called the county rescue unit – and my niece. Apparently, my blood pressure dropped, and I passed out. The doctors determined that my sodium level was too low and my blood pressure medication aggravated things. After a series of tests, my doctor told me, "You need more salt in your diet to raise your blood pressure."

My niece arrived two days ago and has taken charge. Upon release from the hospital, unlike last year, I could leave the hospital with her in the van that Leroy made available. Leroy had my Rollator Walker waiting for me in the breezeway. There was no reception committee waiting for me; Leroy waved from behind his desk, Harvey was in his office with Jane saving him from his latest blunder, and the Geezers were in the study, solving the world's problems.

Barb and I headed to study, "Sorry to disturb your deliberations," I said as I took my 'assigned' seat, "I'm back. Charlie, can you make some room for Barb?  Thank you.  I think we owe her an update on all that has transpired since her daughter's visit earlier this year."

"Wanda was amazing," said Gerald. "Okay, an update. I'm guessing Wand told you about how her meetings with the judge and the Mayor went. When she left, the threat of eminent domain was off the table. *La Petit Refuge* would not become the site for a new condo, but it's strange that nothing has been heard from Rodger Wilkins."

The probate court assigned the property to the city since no beneficiary stepped forward. Wanda convinced the county to convert *La Petit Refuge* into an apartment co-op, with the county sitting on the owner's board. The county got 49 percent of the voting stock. The residents would create a resident council that voted 49 percent of the voting stock.

Everyone agreed Harvey, despite being a twit, was an excellent manager. He was retained as manager and in control of the remaining 2 percent of the voting stock."

"Who funds this enterprise?" asked Barb.

"Well, that's the beauty of it," said Pete. "Monthly rentals collected from the residents are enough to cover operating costs and routine maintenance. This includes salaries, including Harvey's, although I still think we are paying him too much. Major maintenance expenses are covered by the county using a HUD low-income, senior housing grant."

"The resident council is composed of ten members voted on by the residents," I said.

"Their tenure is for one year. We held the first election last month JB and Gerald are council members," said Pete.

"Before you ask, if a council member's mental alertness becomes questionable, they can be removed from the council if seven fellow council members vote for their removal," said Gerald. "We're keeping a close check on JB here," he said with a smile.

As the Geezers were about to break for the day, Leroy came in. "JB, you got an important-looking letter from the Justice Department in the morning mail."

Uncle Joe took the envelope, opened it, and started to laugh. Everyone was looking at him.

"It's a $10k check, the reward money for finding Sean Boyle."

# The End